THE S_____

ON THE STAIRS

AND OTHER SCARY TALES

By Michael Dahl

Illustrated by
Xavier Bonet

raintree
a Capstone company — publishers for children

CONTENTS

Dear Reader,

DO YOU WANT TO KNOW A SECRET?

Everyone is afraid.

Here's another secret: everyone is afraid of different things.

You might be afraid of snakes, spiders, lifts, wardrobes, loud noises, the shadow under your bed. You never know what your friend or the person down the street fears, but one thing is certain – we have all been afraid at one time or another. Fear is something we all have in common.

The following tales also have something in common. They are each about people who are afraid. Very afraid. Read their stories. See if you share their fears.

Because if you don't now ... you will.

Michael Dahl

KNOCK, KNOCK

Noah and his older brother, Sky, both folded their arms and stared at their parents across the dinner table.

"I don't believe it," said Sky.

"You only have to share a bedroom for a week," their mother explained patiently.

"I want my own room," Sky said, pouting.

"As soon as we are finished painting," said their father, "you will each have your own room."

"This place is creepy," said Noah.

Their mother sighed and said, "It's not creepy. There's so much sunshine and fresh air."

It's got sunshine, thought Noah, *because there aren't any trees.*

Their new home had been a boarding house for loggers a hundred years ago. It sat in the middle of boggy fields. The trees for many kilometres around had all been cut down. There was nothing around but whispering cattails and jabbering frogs. The drive was dirt, and it didn't meet another road for at least eight kilometres. The giant house had four porches, a front parlour with five sofas, a sauna built into the side of a hill and more than a dozen bedrooms.

Creepy, Noah had decided.

That night, the brothers trudged angrily up to the third floor of the new house and got ready for bed. Sky rested his head on his pillow and stared over at his brother's bed. "I hope the ghosts don't keep you awake," he said, smiling.

Noah could see his brother's teeth shine in the darkness. "Shut up, Sky," he said.

"Oh, you didn't know?" said Sky. "Yeah, Dad told me this place is haunted."

"I said, shut up!"

"One of the old loggers died outside during a blizzard," Sky continued. "He went out for a wee, and the door locked behind him."

"I mean it!"

"He knocked and knocked," Sky said, "but no one heard him. The wind was too loud. And in the morning, they found him dead on the doorstep, frozen solid."

"Yeah, right." Noah rolled his eyes. He didn't believe his brother at all.

"His hand was frozen in midair," Sky continued. "Like he was trying to knock."

"I'm telling Dad in the morning if you don't stop," said Noah.

"Morning is a long way away," said Sky. Then he snapped off the bedside lamp they both shared and turned over to sleep. "Well, good night, bro."

Noah didn't say anything. He gripped the covers and listened to the wind as it rumbled across the ancient roof.

It's June. There's no chance of a blizzard, Noah thought.

He grew tired, and he finally drifted off to sleep.

But in the middle of the night, he woke up with a start. What was that noise? *Just the wind again,* Noah told himself.

Why did Sky have to tell me that stupid story about the dead logger anyway? Noah wondered. *Even if there was a ghost, what would he be doing up here on the third floor? He'd still be outside, knocking on the door where he died . . . right?* He took a deep breath and leaned back on his pillow.

Tomorrow night, Noah decided, *I'll tell Sky a spooky story. A story about a ghost with burning eyes. Let him try to sleep peacefully tonight, though–*

Knock, knock.

Noah slowly peered over his covers.

Knock, knock.

The sound came from their half-open door.

"Cut it out, Sky," said Noah. He glanced over towards his brother. It was hard to see in the dim moonlight, but it looked like Sky's bed was empty.

Knock, knock.

Noah stared at the door. A shadow stood in the corridor. Tall and heavy, like their father. It didn't move.

"Dad?" croaked Noah. His tongue and lips felt dry.

The shadow grew darker, then faded away. Noah blinked a few times. *My eyes are tired,* he thought. *That's all.*

"Sky," he called weakly.

He heard another sound. Not exactly a knock, but ... more like a bump. And it came from beyond Sky's bed. It came from their wardrobe.

Noah was angry now. This was too much.

He threw off his blankets and jumped up out of bed. He stomped over to the wardrobe and yanked open the door. "Ha, ha! Funny, Sky!" he said.

On the floor of the wardrobe sat his brother. Sky was hunched up, holding his knees to his chest and staring up at Noah in terror. His mouth opened a few times, but nothing came out. Then Sky whispered, "Don't – don't let it in."

Noah felt something grip his shoulder. A cold, hard hand.

COLD SEAT

It was the thing Jake hated more than anything else about winter: a cold toilet seat.

And tonight, that was exactly what he had to look forward to.

His parents and older sister were at a family get-together for New Year's Eve. Jake had refused to go. There had been a big fight, and he ended up staying at home alone. When his family drove off, Jake called his friend Phil, who was planning to have a group of people over. Phil didn't pick up. Jake tried a few other numbers, but no one answered.

Everyone was out having a good time.

A warm time.

Jake's dad insisted on keeping their thermostat set at 17 degrees Celsius. "It saves money," he always said.

But whenever the heat was set at 17 degrees, the toilet seat was freezing. Jake didn't care how much money it cost to keep his bottom warm, but his dad never backed down. And if Jake turned up the heat while his parents were at the party, he knew they'd find out somehow. They always did.

And now Jake had to go to the toilet.

He had been watching the late news on TV, watching all the parties that were happening around the world. Happening without him.

A reporter came on and aired a story about local break-ins. Most houses were empty that evening because their owners were out celebrating all night. It was prime time for burglars and thieves. Some of them could be dangerous.

Just what I need to hear, thought Jake as he pressed the remote.

No matter how many times he switched channels, though, he couldn't switch off the call of nature. And the longer he waited, the colder it would be. That toilet seat would be good and frosty. Especially as he was home alone, and there was no one around to use it before him and warm it up.

Jake trudged down the dark corridor to the bathroom. He prepared himself for the chill against his tender skin. Sitting on the cool seat always reminded him of jumping into a pool full of cold water. Or falling into a snow bank.

Grow up, he thought as he entered the dark bathroom. He didn't flick on the light switch, because he never did. The little moon-shaped nightlight over the sink was usually enough to see by.

Gently, Jake lowered himself onto the seat.

He gasped.

And not because of the cold.

The seat was warm. Nice and warm. As if someone had just been sitting there.

The shower curtain rustled.

CLOSER
AND
CLOSER

As soon as Maddie saw the black bag, she knew something was wrong.

It looked like an ordinary black plastic bin bag. The bigger size, the kind you could stuff leaves inside. But Maddie was certain this bag wasn't holding leaves.

Maddie saw it from the bus on her way to school. She was sitting in her usual seat halfway back on the right-hand side of the bus. And she saw the bag before anyone else got on. Because her house on the east edge of town was the farthest one in the school district, she had a few extra minutes alone each morning before the bus filled up with chattering kids.

She liked staring out of the bus window, watching the scenery ... warehouses, abandoned shops, empty car parks. Maddie planned to be an artist one day. Artists, she knew, were good observers. They saw things that other people missed.

The black bag was at the far end of an empty car park. Maddie noticed it straight away because she looked for that car park every day. She had always liked it because it was covered with grass and delicate white flowers. What was a bag doing there? The bag was lying on its side. It was about half a metre high, with a piece of red yarn tied at one end. Maddie frowned. Someone had dumped their rubbish at the abandoned car park. They must have done it at night when no one was looking.

Some people are just horrible, Maddie thought.

On the bus journey back from school that day, Maddie counted each stop. She counted each child as they left the bus. Finally, when she was the last passenger, Maddie quickly moved to the other side. She wanted to face the empty car park when they passed it again.

Something about the bag bothered her. It had bothered her all day at school. The dark shape was like a smudge on a beautiful painting of grass and flowers. The artist in Maddie hated things that were out of place. That didn't belong.

Finally, the car park was coming into view. Maddie gasped.

Someone had moved the black bag. Maddie was sure she'd seen it at the end of the car park. Now it was in the middle.

Maddie dreamed about the bag that night. And on the bus the following morning, she waited impatiently for the overgrown car park to come into view. When they drove by, the bag had moved again. This time it was lying closer to the street.

Every day that week when Maddie looked for the bag, she saw that it had moved closer and closer to the bus.

On Friday morning, it was so much closer that Maddie got her best view of it. The bag was ... *lumpy*. It looked like it held something heavy. Too heavy to be pushed by the wind.

So a person must have moved it, Maddie thought. *But who would move rubbish around instead of just picking it up?*

That day, Maddie's lessons dragged on forever. On the bus journey home, when the other passengers were gone, Maddie slipped across the aisle. She waited for the grassy car park to appear. Rain slid against the windows, making it harder to see outside. She squinted through the glass. There was the car park coming up. The bus slowed down for a red light.

Maddie shook her head. The bag was gone. The black shape had disappeared. There was nothing but wet grass and flowers. Maddie pressed her forehead against the window and gazed down as far as she could. It wasn't on the pavement or by the drain.

She leaned back against the seat and sighed. So much better. Someone else must have seen the bag and taken it away. Now Maddie's car park wasn't spoiled.

At her bus stop, Maddie picked up her backpack and climbed down the steps to the pavement. The clouds were breaking apart.

Sunshine gleamed off nearby puddles. Maddie was careful to step back from the kerb so she wouldn't get splashed.

As the bus pulled away, a fresh wind blew into Maddie's face.

Then she saw it. It had been hidden by the bus before. But now, across the street, on top of the drain, lay the black bag with the red yarn tied at one end.

Maddie opened her mouth, but nothing came out. She took a few steps back, unable to take her eyes off the bag. Ever so slowly, the bag rolled over and moved towards her. She took a few more steps. The bag rolled again.

Maddie ran to her house.

She refused to look behind her. She raced to the back door and into the kitchen.

Her mother stood at the kitchen counter. "What in the world–" she began.

Maddie dashed past her. She ran down the corridor, into her room. She shut the door behind her, breathing hard.

She was away from the street. Away from the wet and the gutters. Away from that horrible plastic thing.

Maddie took another deep breath, shuddering. The rubbish bin next to her dressing table rustled. The plastic lining inside the bin crinkled. A black shiny lump rose from the bin's mouth as if it were blowing a bubble made of tar. It oozed over the side and onto the pink carpet. It stretched across the floor, longer and longer. A dark, oily cocoon. Then the cocoon curled up, coiling like a cobra, until it touched the ceiling of Maddie's room.

It was a dark serpent, ready to strike.

* * *

The next morning, Cara sat on the bus on the way to school. She was the first passenger. She wondered where that girl called Maddie was. Maddie was always on the bus before her. First one on, last one off. Maybe she was ill.

Cara gazed out of the dirty windows, lost in thought. The bus pulled up to a stoplight. Cara looked out at an empty car park she'd never noticed before. It was covered with grass and tiny white flowers. *It's like a pretty painting,* thought Cara. But something seemed out of place. At the far end of the car park lay something dark. Cara squinted. If only she were closer. It looked like a black plastic bin bag.

No, she was wrong.

There were two.

THE LAVA
GAME

Cory was trying to be a good brother. He was trying very hard. But this was too much.

His little brother, Kyle, and his friends were upstairs yelling in the living room.

"Stay off the floor!"

"Quick! Jump on the sofa!"

"No, don't go that way. You'll fall in the lava and die!"

Cory rolled his eyes. *Kids still play that silly game?* he thought.

The point of the Lava Game was to pretend that the carpet or floor was really hot, molten lava. If you took one wrong step, you could die a painful, fiery death. The living room was the best place to play the Lava Game. It had lots of sofas and chairs and tables to step on, crawl over, climb up and leap to over the lava.

Cory was trying to concentrate on his video game downstairs, but he could still hear their annoying little voices through the floorboards.

Why had he even volunteered to babysit Kyle and his friends? Kyle was eight – old enough to be on his own. He didn't need a thirteen-year-old telling him what to do. But now Cory was getting annoyed. He was busy fighting off a shipload of alien soldiers, and Kyle and his friends were being too loud.

Cory ran upstairs.

"Keep it down, you little creeps!" he shouted. He planted himself in the archway to the living room. Kyle and his friends froze. They each stood on a different piece of furniture.

"We're trying to survive here," said Kyle, waving his arms.

"Yeah," echoed one of his friends. Cory thought the boy's name was Bree or Ree or something. "We can't die!" the boy said.

"I can't believe you lot still play that game," Cory said with a smirk.

"It's not a game," said Kyle. "It's life or death!"

"I thought you'd have outgrown playing Lava by now," said Cory.

Kyle and his friends looked at one another. "What's Lava?" asked Bree or Ree.

Cory had taken a few steps into the living room. It was too late.

"It's quicksand!" yelled Kyle. "The floor is quicksand."

Cory didn't realize what was happening until he had sunk up to his knees in the thick green carpet. He could feel something warm and mushy. It felt like half mud, half pudding.

Kyle and his friends screamed. "Get out! Get out!"

Cory was so startled he couldn't speak. He flailed his arms, looking for something solid to grab on to. Now he was up to his chest. He was too far from any furniture.

"Kyle," he cried. "Help!"

Kyle looked around, helpless. Then he pulled up one of the cushions from the sofa he stood on. He threw it towards his brother who grabbed it with both hands. Cory held onto it but the cushion sank into the carpet like a cracker in hot soup.

The thick carpet was up to Cory's chin.

"What do we do?!" yelled Bree or Ree.

"I can't reach him!" screamed Kyle.

"Stay off the floor! You'll fall in and sink too!" cried another friend.

"Cory!"

Cory sank out of sight, his hands grasping at the air.

The carpet closed over him. It was smooth and still, as if nothing had ever been there. A part of the carpet bunched up suddenly into a small bump, a bubble. Then it was gone.

"My mother's going to kill me," moaned Kyle.

LOVE BUG

"The average human swallows seventeen spiders while they sleep. Did you know that?" Doug asked, his eyes shining with excitement.

"Uh, no," said Laura.

"But that's spread out over a lifetime," added Doug. "Since we're only fourteen, we've lived, like, maybe a sixth of our lives. So we've probably only swallowed two or three by now."

"Good to know," Laura replied.

"It doesn't bother me, though," said Doug. "Since I'm a–"

They both finished his sentence together: "–bug person."

Doug sighed happily and continued to stare up at the moon.

Laura stared at Doug, then down at her hands in her lap. She was wearing her new sky-blue dress. She and her mother had bought it for the school dance. Doug hadn't said anything about it.

Maybe, Laura thought, *if it had been decorated with beetles or centipedes or millipedes – maybe then, Doug would have noticed.*

At least he was nice. And he looked cute in his polo shirt and tie.

"Why are you letting Doug the Bug take you to the dance?" her shocked friends had all asked her earlier that week.

"Buggy Dougie is creepy," her friend Vanda had said.

"I wouldn't say creepy," her other friend Caroline had said. "But he *is* a nerd. A bug nerd. Yuck."

"A cute nerd," Laura had said quietly.

Besides, the boy she had hoped would ask her to the dance, Powell, hadn't said a word to her all week. Nothing. He hadn't showed up at the dance that night either. Neither had his friends. They probably thought it was stupid.

More likely, thought Laura, *they just didn't have the guts to ask a girl out.*

Boys were odd creatures, Laura knew. An entirely different species from girls.

At least Doug had asked her. He was nice, too. He had danced with her, not well, but he'd tried. And he'd sat next to her when they ate and talked. Mostly about bugs.

"So, what were those millipedes you talked about before?" Laura asked.

They were sitting on a bench just a couple of streets from school. Doug had offered to walk Laura home. They had decided to take a shortcut through the park. Then Laura had suggested they sit by the lake for a bit. The smooth water shone in the full moonlight like an icy skating rink. The air was warm and still.

"Yeah," Doug replied. "'Millepede' means a thousand feet. But they don't really have a thousand. They have lots of them, though.

Dozens. They can even have, like, three hundred feet!"

"I never knew that," said Laura.

"Yes," said Doug, his face shining in the moonlight. "They're amazing creatures. In fact, they're my favourite. If I ever came back in another life, I'd want to come back as a millipede."

"Oh," said Laura.

"But some of them are poisonous," Doug explained. "So I'd have to be careful."

"Right."

"How about you?" Doug asked. "What would you want to come back as?"

Laura thought for a moment. No one had ever asked her that question. "Hmm, maybe a deer. Or a gazelle," she said. "Something graceful."

"Yeah, gazelles are beautiful," said Doug.

He sighed happily again, and this time he reached over and took Laura's hand. She let him. It felt nice, sitting in the moonlight with a cute boy. Just sitting and holding hands and talking. Even if they were talking about millipedes. Even if the boy was Doug the Bug.

Laura looked up at the Moon and smiled.

She felt Doug's hand in hers. Then he put his other hand around her waist. And his other hand wrapped around her shoulder, and his other hand held out a flower, and his other hand brushed her hair back, and...

UNDER
COVERS

I love comics.

Especially the old-timey ones like my grandpa collects. Whenever I stay overnight at Grandpa's house, he drags out these big plastic crates from his back room. He calls the room his office, but it's more like a room-sized junk drawer. He plops the crates down, snaps off the plastic lids, and shows me his favourites.

"Here's the first Amazing Spider-Man issue," he says. "And not the one in the films. I mean the real deal, the original. See? Here he is, trapped by the Fantastic Four."

"Cool," I say. And it is. The Human Torch, another hero, is flaming across the cover. He's in the Fantastic Four's headquarters, and Spider-Man is caught inside a big glass tube. This Spider-Man has webs hanging from his arms. Never saw that before!

Each comic book is inside a thin plastic cover that seals at the top. Grandpa says it protects the paper from ageing and falling apart. Too bad they couldn't do that with people. If you could do that with people, when Grandpa got older, I could put him inside one and take him out on special occasions.

Grandpa puts the Spider-Man comic back in the crate carefully. He must have hundreds in there. All stacked up like individual slices of plastic-wrapped cheese.

"Aha! Here's one you haven't read before!" Grandpa says. He sounds like he's just discovered buried treasure. "Superman gets trapped in the far future when the Sun grows old and turns red!"

That's bad. Everyone knows Superman has no powers under a red sun.

At night, before bed, Grandpa always lets me choose two comics to read by myself. "But you

can't lie down. You have to sit up," he orders.
"Otherwise, you'll fall asleep and roll over on
the comic."

I don't blame him for wanting to be extra
careful. Some of those old comics are worth
loads of money. I looked up that first Spider-
Man issue online. If Grandpa ever sold it, he
could make a fortune!

Tonight, I'm right in the middle of my second
comic, a Legion of Super-Heroes adventure.

"Ten o'clock!" Grandpa yells from the hall.
"Lights out!"

Grandpa is strict about his lights-out rule.
Even if I'm in the middle of a comic, I have to
turn off the light.

Which is why, for this visit, I brought a mini-
torch with me.

I flip off the light and wait. I count to one
hundred. I reckon Grandpa will be in bed by
now himself. Yup, I can hear him snoring.

I crawl under the covers and switch on the
torch. It's perfect. It's like hiding in a tent. I
finish the Legion adventure. Element Lad saves

his fellow Legionnaires by turning the bad guy's feet into uranium, the heaviest element on Earth!

My eyes are droopy, and it's a little stuffy under the covers. I switch off the light and crawl back towards the pillows. Funny. I can't feel the edge of the sheet above me. So then I crawl what feels like three metres. The bed itself is only two metres long.

I crawl further. I still can't find the end. What is going on?

I switch the torch back on. I try standing up, but the sheet above me is heavy, like the roof of a tent. I can barely rise up on my knees, pushing against the sheet with my head and reaching out with one arm to make as much space as possible. I swing the light back and forth. No sight of the end of the sheet. No pillows. No bed. I don't see the other comic, either – the first one I had read.

This is crazy. I try a different direction. Maybe I can reach the side of the bed and crawl out.

That doesn't work either. I must crawl for ten whole minutes, and I never reach the end. How can a sheet be this long? What happened to the bed? Where is Grandpa?

"Grandpa!" I yell. No answer. Maybe he can't hear me under this fabric. I yell some more, but I never hear him answer.

So I crawl towards what I think is the foot of the bed. I move as fast as I can. It's hard moving fast on a soft, lumpy bed – even a bed as long and wide as this one seems to be – with a comic in one hand and a torch in the other. I put my head down like an angry bull and plough forwards as fast as I can. I'll probably crash into the wooden wall at the foot of the bed, but I don't care. Escaping into the fresh air is worth a bruised skull.

No such luck. I crawl and crawl for hours.

The torch won't last much longer. The batteries will give out soon.

Then I see it. A light in the distance. The edge of the bed!

As I crawl towards the light, it seems to change. It looks less and less like light peeping under the edge of a sheet and more like a car's headlights down a long dark street. I crawl closer. The beam grows smaller and sharper. Another torch!

It's another boy crawling towards *me*.

In his other hand, he holds a comic. Three or four other boys are crawling right behind him.

"Who are you?" he asks.

"What do you mean, 'who are you'?" I say. "What are you lot doing in my bed?"

"Your bed?" comes a muffled voice from behind the torch-leader-boy.

The torch boy snorts. "You don't get it," he says. "This ain't anybody's bed. I don't know what it is, but it ain't a bed."

"We've been trying to find a way out since last night," says a boy at the back.

"Since two nights ago!" says another.

The leader gives me a look. "I don't know how long we've been in here," he says. "All I know is I was reading a comic under the covers with my torch–"

"And when you tried to crawl out, this is where you ended up," I say.

He nods.

"I was reading Spider-Man," moans a boy in the back.

"Iron Man, a double issue," says another.

"I'm hungry!" groans a third.

How many boys are here, anyway? I wonder.

The torch boy shouts over his shoulder to his followers. "If we stay in one direction we'll have to find a way out." Then he looks at me and says, in a whisper, "It can't go on forever, right?"

"Uh, right," I say, not knowing if I'm right or wrong. But I guess I'll find out soon enough.

So I crawl along with the others, holding out my light.

Before long, we come across an abandoned pile of comics. Old ones. Just like Grandpa has. I mean, these ones are vintage and worth a lot of money. Superman. Batman. Green Lantern. The Hulk.

We all get excited. We reach out to pick up the comics, but the pages crumble.

"Wha – what happened?" asks one child.

"They were old," says another. "Like they've been here forever."

Everyone's quiet. We're probably all thinking the same thing. Forever is a long time.

"We gotta keep moving," says their leader.

So on we go. Crawling and crawling.

The torches are growing dim.

THE
STRANGER
ON THE
STAIRS

Six-year-old Brandon Spode hated climbing the stairs at night.

"Time for bed, Brandon," said his mother. "Up to your room."

"I don't want to," Brandon moaned.

"Don't tell me it's the man again," said Mrs Spode.

"He's sitting up there," said Brandon.

Mrs Spode stood at the bottom of the stairs, her hands on her hips, and looked up. "There's nothing there," she said.

Mrs Spode had braces on her legs, so she never climbed the stairs herself. Her bedroom was on the main floor.

Brandon pointed. "He's right there."

"That's a shadow," said Mrs Spode. "The light in the hall makes a shadow. You know what a shadow is, don't you?"

Brandon nodded. He knew what a shadow was. But he also knew that the man on the stairs wasn't made by light and shadows.

The man sat there every night on the top step. His skin was the colour of a red crayon that had melted on the pavement. His eyebrows were thick and bushy. He had a wide grin that stretched his face tight, like the skin of a balloon. Three reddish bumps grew on his forehead.

"I don't want to go to bed," said Brandon.

Mrs Spode was tired of having the same argument every night. "This time I'll stand right here and watch you go up the stairs," she said. "All right?"

Brandon didn't move.

"It's getting late, young man," his mother said.

Slowly, Brandon took the first step.

The man on the stairs never moved. When Brandon had first seen him, he thought the man was a statue. But when he passed him, Brandon could hear breathing. Then one night, he saw the man blink.

"Hurry up, Brandon. I can't stand here all night, can I?" said Mrs Spode.

The boy approached the figure on the top step.

"Keep going," said his mother.

Brandon heard breathing. He could see white teeth gleaming in the stretched-out grin.

The boy shut his eyes. He kept climbing. He put his right hand against the wall to guide him. Brandon stumbled a bit when his feet reached the landing. He was at the top. He opened his eyes and looked down at his mother.

"See, I told you," said Mrs Spode, crossing her arms. "There's no man sitting on the stairs, now is there?"

"No," Brandon said softly.

"Then get to bed," ordered his mother. The woman turned and saw a man standing behind her. A man with a red face, bumps on his forehead, and a wide, stretchy smile.

Upstairs, Brandon heard a scream and then a thud as his mother fainted and hit the floor.

ABOUT THE AUTHOR

Michael Dahl, the author of the Library of Doom and Troll Hunters series, is an expert on fear. He is afraid of heights (but he still flies). He is afraid of small, enclosed spaces (but his house is crammed with over 3,000 books). He is afraid of ghosts (but that same house is haunted). He hopes that by writing about fear, he will eventually be able to overcome his own. So far it is not working. But he is afraid to stop. He claims that, if he had to, he would travel to Mount Doom in order to toss in a dangerous piece of jewellery. Even though he is afraid of volcanoes. And jewellery.

ABOUT THE ILLUSTRATOR

Xavier Bonet is an illustrator and comic-book
artist who resides in Barcelona. Experienced in
2D illustration, he has worked as an animator
and a background artist for several different
production companies. He aims to create works
full of colour, texture and sensation, using
both traditional and digital tools. His work in
children's literature is inspired by magic and
fantasy as well as his passion for the art.

MICHAEL DAHL TELLS ALL

Readers often ask me where I get my ideas. To be honest, I don't always know! Sometimes the ideas arrive on the doorstep of my imagination all dressed up and say, "You were expecting us, right?" Other times they come in dreams, quietly and politely. Still others come when I brainstorm with friends, write down sentences in a notebook or take a long walk. Here's where the stories in this book came from.

KNOCK, KNOCK

When I was a boy, my aunt and her five daughters lived in an old house in northern Minnesota, USA, that was once a hotel for loggers. It was gigantic and isolated, with a dark, crumbly sauna built underneath. My mum and sisters and I would visit them for several weeks during the summer holidays. We spent the evenings telling scary stories and watching *Twilight Zone* on TV.

When I started thinking about scary stories to write, the old loggers' lodge seemed like the perfect setting for a ghost story. I combined that with the truly scary winters we get in Minnesota, where some people have indeed frozen to death while accidentally locked outside their homes.

CLOSER AND CLOSER

I took the bus to school. Then I took a bus to university, and then to work. I spent a lot of time on buses observing people, overhearing strange conversations and staring out of the window. Buses don't seem like scary places at all, which made me want to write a story about one. One thing that does creep me out: **black plastic bin bags**. They look like slug monsters. Blob creatures. I don't like how the plastic feels either. And who knows what's *really* inside those bags?

COLD SEAT

I had just moved into my new house, and I was coming out of the upstairs bathroom one night when I saw the ghost for the first time. Yes, I live in a haunted house. The ghost's name is **Helen**, by the way. Since then, I've found bathrooms ... unsettling. While on the subject of toilets, my friend and fellow writer Donnie Lemke suggested that a warm seat is worse than a cold seat – for the very reason that comes up in the story.

THE LAVA GAME

Do you play the Lava Game? Sometimes my friends and I called it the **Poison Game**. My mother didn't like the game, whatever it was called, because we bounced all over her good furniture. We never considered quicksand, because that would be too hard to act out. It was easy to pretend you were being burned up by lava or had been poisoned – you simply screamed loudly and then fell over. But how could you sink down into a rug? This story was a way of finding out what might happen.

LOVE BUG

My friend Donnie strikes again! He and I were chatting about how creepy it would be for humans to turn into **centipedes**, and – voilà! – the story was born. (Isn't it nice having friends who you can talk to about anything?) As I was writing, I thought it would be even worse if the half-human, half-insect was someone you really liked.

UNDER COVERS

I've spent many school nights under the covers with a torch and a comic book. I still **read comics in bed**, though now I'm old enough that I don't need anyone's permission. One night when I was a boy, I had been reading a terrific story about the Legion of Super Heroes, and for some reason I got all twisted up under the sheets. It took me a few seconds to realize I was heading in the wrong direction, towards the foot of the bed. But recently, as I thought about those long-ago nights, I wondered what would have happened if I *hadn't* found the way out. Then what? A lot of good stories spring into shape when you simply ask, "What if...?"

THE STRANGER ON THE STAIRS

This tale was the result of a challenge I gave myself: What's the **creepiest story** I can write using the least amount of words?

GLOSSARY

abandoned left behind; forgotten

ageing becoming older

annoying pestering

boggy wet and muddy

braces devices used to support a weak leg, arm or other body part

concentrate give all your thought and attention to something

dangerous not safe

delicate finely made; sensitive

droopy hanging down; sagging

jabbering talking quickly

molten melting at a high temperature

smudge blur or smear on something

species one the groups into which animals and plants are divided

thermostat device that controls the temperature of heating and cooling systems

volunteered offered to do a job without pay

DISCUSSION QUESTIONS

1. I was inspired to write "Knock, Knock" by my aunt's home, an old lodge for loggers in northern Minnesota, USA. Have you been somewhere that scared you? Talk about how you could make it into a story.

2. In "Cold Seat", Jake is terrified that someone has broken into his home – and used the toilet! Do you think someone is in Jake's house? Discuss why or why not.

3. In the story "Closer and Closer", Cara notices that there are two bin bags in an empty car park that her school bus passes each morning. Where do you think the two bin bags came from? Talk about the possibilities.

WRITING PROMPTS

1. Pick one story from this book and write a different ending for it – but make sure it's scary!

2. Imagine you are Buggy Dougie in the story "Love Bug". Write a version of the story from his point of view.

3. A lot of scary stories involve ghosts. Do you believe in ghosts? Write a paragraph explaining why or why not.

MICHAEL DAHL'S
REALLY SCARY STORIES